Can You Keep a Secret?

Can You Keep a Secret?

P. J. Petersen

illustrated by

MEREDITH JOHNSON

DUTTON CHILDREN'S BOOKS

NEW YORK

Library of Congress Cataloging-in-Publication Data
Petersen, P. J.
Can you keep a secret?/by P. J. Petersen; illustrated by
Meredith Johnson.—1st ed.   p.   cm.
Summary: Mike has a reputation for not being able to keep a secret,
and he worries that he may reveal things that his classmates
do not want known—from a surprise party for one of the teachers
to a snake in a friend's desk.
ISBN 0-525-45840-9
[1. Schools—Fiction.   2. Secrets—Fiction.]
I. Johnson, Meredith, ill.   II. Title.
PZ7.P44197Sej   1997   [Fic]—DC21   97-6148   CIP   AC

Published in the United States by Dutton Children's Books,
a division of Penguin Books USA Inc.
375 Hudson Street, New York, New York 10014
Designed by Ellen M. Lucaire
Printed in USA   First Edition
1   3   5   7   9   10   8   6   4   2

21219

For my daughter Carla
P.J.P.

For Alex, a great secret-keeper
M.J.

Can You Keep a Secret?

Chapter One

Mike ran across the playground, bouncing a big red ball. He felt great. They had fifteen minutes to play wall-ball before school started.

Nate and Sam were bent over, looking at something. "Watch out," Nate said. "Here comes Mike." Sam turned his back and put something into his coat pocket.

"What's in your pocket, Sam?" Mike asked.

"Nothing," Sam said.

"Come on," Mike said. "You can tell me."

Sam shook his head. "No way. You can't keep a secret."

"I won't tell," Mike said.

Nate laughed. "Yes, you will. You won't mean to. But you'll tell just the same."

Mike stamped over to the wall-ball court. He was mad. What Sam said was sort of true. Mike wasn't very good at keeping secrets. It was hard to know a secret and not tell somebody.

And sometimes, even when he didn't want to tell, he gave away secrets by accident.

Even so, he didn't like his friends hiding things from him.

Mike put the ball on the ground by the DO NOT KICK BALLS sign. He kicked the ball hard. Harder than he meant to. The ball sailed clear over the wall. It even went over the net that was supposed to catch high balls. Mike heard it bounce on the roof.

Mike ran to the side of the building. He waited for the ball to roll off the roof. But it didn't. It must be stuck up there. And Mike was in trouble again.

But maybe not. Maybe nobody had seen him.

Mike looked around quickly. People were busy playing two-square and tetherball. Some older girls were standing in a big circle and giggling. The only person close by was Amy. She was carrying a vase full of flowers.

"Hi, Amy," Mike called.

Amy waved to him.

"Did you see what happened to me?" he asked.

"No," Amy said. "What happened?"

"I just had a little accident," Mike said, walking away. He was safe.

But his stomach felt funny. Like he'd eaten too many pancakes.

Nate came running across the playground. "Let's play wall-ball," he said.

"We can't," Mike said.

Nate looked around. "Where's the ball?"

"Don't tell anybody," Mike said. "I kicked it, and it got stuck on the roof."

"Mr. Warren's on yard duty," Nate said. "Maybe you should go tell him right now."

"I'll get in trouble," Mike said.

Nate shrugged. "He'll find out anyway."

"Maybe he won't," Mike said. But he had that bad feeling in his stomach.

They walked across the playground, past some first-grade girls jumping rope. The girls were shouting out their rhyme:

You are ugly.
You have germs.
You should eat
A can of worms.

Mike saw Sam in a circle with some older kids. "What's Sam doing?" Mike asked.

"Forget it," Nate said. "Let's shoot some baskets with Fred." Fred was the best basketball player in the class. He lived next door to the school, and he was always playing ball.

"Did Sam bring another frog to school?" Mike asked.

6

"No," Nate said. "But remember what happened that time."

"It wasn't my fault," Mike said. "I was just holding it for a second, and Mrs. Banks caught me."

"You know why she caught you?"

"Maybe somebody told," said Mike.

"All she had to do was look at your face," Nate said. "One look, and she knew you were up to something."

"Hey," Fred yelled, "you guys want me to whip you in a little game?"

Mike and Nate played Fred in basketball, two against one. But Fred still beat them. While they played, Mike kept looking across the playground at Sam. Sam and another boy were down on their knees, playing with something.

The first bell rang. "Fourteen to ten," Fred said. "I told you I'd whip you."

Mr. Warren was standing by the steps. Mike's knees got shaky. Now his stomach felt like he had swallowed cement.

"Let's wait," Mike told Nate. "We'll go in just before the second bell."

When they came close to the steps, Mike got on the other side of Nate. That way, Nate was between him and Mr. Warren. Mike kept his head down. He wouldn't look at Mr. Warren at all.

Ahead of Nate and Mike, some sixth-grade girls were singing. One girl was dancing to the music. "I wish you were on the radio," a boy yelled. "Then I could turn you off."

Mike felt a little better. With so many kids around, Mr. Warren wouldn't even notice him.

The girl in front of him was wearing purple tennis shoes. She had written something on the soles in green ink. Mike watched those shoes go up the first step. And the second. He put his foot on the first step.

"Mike," Mr. Warren called out.

Mike went up another step. He'd pretend he didn't hear.

"Mike!" Mr. Warren shouted.

Nate grabbed Mike's arm. "Mr. Warren wants you."

People moved back and let Mike go past. Then they stood and waited, trying to hear.

"Let's go, Mike," Mr. Warren said. They walked across the empty playground. Mr. Warren stopped by the two-square courts and looked down at Mike. "What's the story?"

"I went out to play wall-ball," Mike said. "But I got mad and kicked the ball. And it went on the roof and got stuck up there. I didn't mean to."

Mr. Warren nodded. "And you didn't tell anybody?"

"No."

"Two mistakes," Mr. Warren said. "What were they?"

"I shouldn't have kicked the ball. And I should have told somebody about the ball on the roof."

Mr. Warren smiled. "Two out of two. You get one hundred percent on the before-school quiz. So you know what you should have done. You just didn't do it."

"How did you know?" Mike asked.

"You had that look on your face," Mr. Warren said. "You stay after school today. Bring your books to my room."

"Okay," Mike said. "I'm sorry."

"You did something stupid," Mr. Warren said. "Everybody does that once in a while. Now hurry up. Try to get to class before the last bell rings."

Mike ran for the steps. He was smiling. He had to stay after school, but that was all right. At least his stomach didn't hurt anymore.

Chapter
Two

Amy watched Mr. Warren take Mike away from the steps. "He's in big trouble," one of the sixth graders said.

Amy felt sorry for Mike. But she was glad Mr. Warren was gone. She knew a secret about Mr. Warren, and she felt funny being around him.

She had kept her secret all to herself since last Friday. Three whole days. It was an exciting secret. And a happy one. She wanted to tell somebody. But she didn't know who.

Before, she could have told Sara. Sara was her best friend, and they told each other everything. But two weeks ago Sara had moved to Arizona. And she hadn't even written Amy a letter yet.

Amy needed a best friend right now. She wanted to talk about what she'd seen. But everybody seemed to have a best friend already.

Amy walked into the classroom. Carla and Britt were whispering in the corner. Amy wished she could go over there and whisper with them.

Some boys were standing around Sam's desk. She wondered what Sam had this time. Last month he'd gotten into trouble for having a frog. And before that he'd had a pet grasshopper.

Amy kept glancing back there, but she couldn't see what it was. Probably another frog. But she wished she knew.

Mrs. Banks was digging through a big stack of papers. She always had piles of papers on her desk and on the bookcases. And she was always losing things. Mrs. Banks was one of the nicest teachers Amy had ever had. But she was also the messiest.

Mrs. Banks looked up from her papers and said, "Thank you for the flowers, Amy. They're beautiful."

Amy often brought flowers to school. Her parents owned a garden shop, and they usually had extra flowers. Amy liked making bouquets and giving them to people.

That's how she had learned her secret. Last week she had brought a bouquet for Mr. Warren's desk. On Friday she was supposed to bring home the vase, but she had forgotten.

After school she'd gone shopping with her mother. On their way home, Amy had remembered the vase. Mr. Warren's car was still in the parking lot, so Amy had run to his room and pulled open the door.

There, inside the room, she had seen the most amazing thing: Mr. Warren kissing Miss Dean, the kindergarten teacher. When they heard Amy, they moved apart very quickly. They acted like nothing had happened. And so did she.

Mr. Warren and Miss Dean! It was such a

surprise. Lots of girls talked about how cute Mr. Warren was. But none of them knew that Miss Dean thought so, too.

Amy wasn't sure about the school rules. Last month some sixth graders had gotten in trouble for holding hands. Amy didn't know if teachers had the same rules. She didn't want to get Mr. Warren in trouble. But something this good—she wanted to talk it over with somebody.

Amy sat down at her desk. Greg, who sat across from her, was already in his seat. "Hi, Greg," she said.

"Hi." Greg didn't look up. He was nice enough. But she only talked to him about school. She'd never talk to him about kissing.

Brenda, who sat behind Amy, marched to the front of the room. "Mrs. Banks," she shouted, "some dirty sneak stole my pencil. It was right in the front of my desk. And now it's gone."

Mrs. Banks looked at Brenda and laughed. "The same dirty sneak hid the reports I want," Mrs. Banks said. She handed Brenda a pencil. "Use this one."

Brenda held up the pencil. "Mine was longer than this. Almost new."

"You're welcome," Mrs. Banks said, reaching for another pile of papers.

The last bell rang. The boys around Sam's desk moved into their seats. Mrs. Banks pushed aside a stack of books and sat on the front of her desk. "Good morning," she said. "This is going to be a special day."

"No math today?" Nate asked.

"Not for a while," Mrs. Banks said.

Everybody cheered. Even Amy, and she loved math.

"I have a secret to tell you about Mr. Warren," Mrs. Banks said.

Amy's mouth dropped open. She couldn't believe what she was hearing. This couldn't be *her* secret. But two secrets about Mr. Warren—that was amazing!

Just then Mike came through the door. "Oh-oh," somebody said, "you'd better not tell Mike. He'll tell the whole school." Lots of people laughed.

Mike's face got red. Amy felt sorry for him. Mike was always nice to her. He was nice to everybody. She didn't like people laughing at him.

"Come and sit down, Mike," Mrs. Banks said. "I was just saying that this is a special day. We're going to plan a surprise party for Mr. Warren. Tomorrow is his birthday."

Amy smiled. She felt better. A surprise party was a good secret. But she knew an even better one.

"How old is he?" Brenda asked.

"That's what makes this special," Mrs. Banks said. "He's going to be thirty."

"I didn't think he was *that* old," one of the boys said.

"Wow," Sam said, "he's as old as my mom."

Amy was surprised too. Mr. Warren didn't seem old to her at all. Sometimes he played tetherball or wall-ball with the kids. He even jumped rope.

"I have an idea," Mrs. Banks said. "You did

wonderful poems for Trent when he was in the hospital. And for Sara when she was leaving. I think it would be great to do birthday poems for Mr. Warren. We'll have a party tomorrow, and you can all read your poems."

"And we're supposed to keep this a secret?" somebody asked.

"I think you can handle that," Mrs. Banks said.

"We better tape Mike's mouth shut," Fred said.

Mike stuck out his tongue.

"Let's go to work," Mrs. Banks said. "And let's try not to do any 'Roses are red' poems. I know you did haiku poems in Mr. Warren's class last week. You might do one of those."

Amy tried to think of a poem. Maybe she'd write one about thirty candles on a cake. Or about having a surprise party. She couldn't decide. She knew one thing her poem wouldn't be about. It would not be about kissing kindergarten teachers.

Chapter Three

The first thing Mike heard when he came through the door was dumb old Trent saying, "You better not tell Mike. He'll tell the whole school." That made Mike mad, but he tried not to show it. He hurried to his desk without looking at anybody.

Mrs. Banks told them about Mr. Warren's birthday. Mike thought the party was a good idea. But he thought writing poems was a lousy idea.

Mike was good at lots of things—drawing, sports, science. And he was great with computers. But he was bad at poems.

Everything he wrote sounded dumb. He knew the kind of poem he wanted to write, but he just couldn't write it. When the class wrote poems, he had to get somebody to help him.

While people were getting out paper, Nate looked back and asked, "Did you get in trouble?"

"Yeah," Mike said. "I have to stay after school."

"It's better than having a note sent home," Nate said. "Last time I got a note, it was no TV for a whole week."

Mike took out a piece of paper. Then he sat and looked at it. He felt really stupid. Everybody else was writing away.

Nate slapped down his pencil and said, "I'm done."

"Let me see it," Mike said. Maybe he could get an idea from Nate.

Nate held up his paper so Mike could read it:

That didn't seem like much of a poem, but Mike said, "That's neat."

Nate looked at Mike's blank paper. "What's the matter? Are you mad at Mr. Warren?"

"I can't think of anything right now," Mike said.

"Give me your paper," Nate said. "I'll write one for you."

"I can do it," Mike said.

But Nate reached back and grabbed his paper. While Nate was writing, Mike looked around the room. He saw Sam raise the lid of his desk and reach inside. Sam was petting something. Mike was sure of it.

"Here you go," Nate said. He set the paper in front of Mike. "It's a good one."

Mike looked at the poem in front of him:

HOPE YOU GET PRESENTS YOU LIKE!!
YOUR FRIEND, MIKE

That sounded dumb to Mike. But he said, "Thanks, Nate. It's neat."

"No problem," Nate said. "As long as you have a good rhyming name. If your name was Charles or Oscar, you'd be out of luck."

Mike felt out of luck anyway. He looked across at Britt's desk. Britt was drawing hearts and flowers around the edges of her paper. Britt always wrote good poems. Maybe he could get an idea from her.

"Britt," he whispered, "can I see your poem?"

"Okay," she said. "But hold it by the edges. I don't want the ink to smear."

Mike took Britt's poem and set it on his desk:

Marvelous
Really nice

Wonderful
Awesome
Really friendly
Really sweet
Exciting
Now you're 30.
HAPPY BIRTHDAY!

"See?" Britt said. "It spells out Mr. Warren."

Britt's poem gave Mike an idea. He could do one like it. He could spell out HAPPY BIRTHDAY. He got out another piece of paper and wrote a big *H* on the first line. Then he tried to think of a good *h* word. But all he could think of was *horse* and *hippo* and *Halloween*. This kind of poem was harder than he thought.

Britt looked over at his paper. "You better not copy my idea," she said.

Mike crumpled up his paper. He'd never be able to think of enough words anyway.

"Is everybody finished?" Mrs. Banks asked.

Mike put Nate's poem in his desk. Tonight he'd try to write a poem for Mr. Warren. But he'd keep Nate's poem just in case.

The class talked about food for the party. "I don't care what kind of cake we get," Fred said. "Just so it has lots of frosting."

Mike didn't listen to the talk. He was watching Sam. Sam still had his hand inside his desk. And he had a big smile on his face.

When the party plans were finished, Mrs. Banks had them get out their math books. Mike worked for a while, then pushed down hard on his pencil and broke the lead. He got up and went to the pencil sharpener.

Mrs. Banks had her back turned. She was looking in the file cabinet.

Mike stopped beside Sam's desk. "Let me see your frog, Sam."

"You're going to get me in trouble," Sam said.

"Let me see it."

Sam took a Hot Tamales candy box out of his desk. He opened one end and stuck a finger inside. "This is Ernie," Sam whispered.

Mike put his hand under the box. He wanted to hold the frog. But a snake came sliding out. Mike yanked his hand back. The snake wasn't as big around as Mike's pencil. But it was still a little scary. Its red tongue kept flicking out.

"You want to pet him?" Sam asked.

Mike didn't. But he reached out a finger. Slowly.

"Mike," Mrs. Banks called out, "what are you doing?"

"I have to sharpen my pencil." Mike hurried down the aisle.

Mrs. Banks looked up at him. Mike felt his stomach get tight. "Make it quick," she said. "And no visiting along the way." She reached into the file cabinet again.

Mike sharpened his pencil and went straight back to his desk. He waved at Ernie

when he went by Sam's desk. But he didn't even slow down.

He wasn't taking any chances. This time he wasn't going to get anybody in trouble. He'd show them he could keep a secret.

Chapter Four

Amy had a hard time writing her poem. As soon as Mrs. Banks told then not to do "Roses are red" poems, she thought of one right away. And she couldn't get it out of her mind:

> *Roses are red.*
> *Grass is green.*
> *I saw you*
> *Kiss Miss Dean.*

Amy held her hand over her mouth to keep from laughing out loud. She wished Sara was here. Sara would love that poem.

Amy and Sara used to make up silly jump rope rhymes. They'd start laughing and forget to jump.

Sitting there at her desk, Amy thought of a jump rope rhyme that Sara would love:

> *Here comes the doctor.*
> *Here comes the preacher.*
> *I saw you kiss*
> *The kindergarten teacher.*

Amy laughed out loud. People turned and looked at her. Amy felt her face get hot. She looked down at the blank paper on her desk.

"What's so funny?" Nate asked her.

"Nothing," Amy said. But she almost laughed out loud again.

"You having trouble thinking of a poem?" Nate asked.

"Sort of," Amy said.

"Listen to mine," Nate said. " 'Hope your birthday's great. Your friend, Nate.' I'd write one for you, but nothing rhymes with *Amy*."

"I'll think of something," Amy said.

Amy saw Sam putting his hand inside his desk. She was sure he had another frog.

Mrs. Banks walked around the room, looking at some of the poems. Amy picked up her pencil. Maybe she'd do a haiku. Haiku were little poems—three lines, seventeen syllables. That wouldn't be hard.

She wrote down a poem, then counted syllables. She had to change some words, but finally it came out right:

> *Mr. Warren smiles*
> *when he eats a giant piece*
> *of pink birthday cake.*

Amy read over her poem. It wasn't bad. But everybody else had probably done a haiku too. She wanted to do something special. She'd try again at home.

While Mrs. Banks talked about the party,

Amy looked back at Sam. She saw him take a little box out of his desk for a minute, then put it back. She wondered what the frog looked like. Maybe if she asked Sam, he'd show it to her.

Then they did math papers. Amy finished hers right away. She was good at numbers. Sometimes, when she was waiting for something, she played number games in her head. There were twenty-six kids in her class. If there were two classes, there would be fifty-two. Three classes would be seventy-eight. Four classes—

Mike got up from his desk. He held his pencil over his head so Mrs. Banks would know what he was doing. But he stopped by Sam's desk. Amy saw Sam take the box out of his desk. And she saw Mike jump back. That surprised her. She didn't think Mike would be afraid of frogs. It must be a really big one.

When the bell rang, Mrs. Banks said, "Okay, it's softball today. Everybody go to the softball field."

"Goody," Carla said. She was great at soft-ball.

"Yuck," Amy said to herself. She hated play-ing softball with the boys. They got mad if you struck out, which she usually did. And they yelled at you and made you nervous. And there were too many players on each team, so ones like Amy ended up in the outfield. What kind of game was that—with six or seven outfielders?

Amy stopped to fix the bouquet on Mrs. Banks's desk. Some of the roses were hang-ing crooked.

"Let's go, Amy," Mrs. Banks said as she went out the door.

"I'll be right there," she said. She kept work-ing on the flowers. Everybody else was gone. She liked being there in the room by herself. It was much better than being out on the softball field. Sometimes it was nice being alone.

Alone! She looked over at Sam's desk. Then she glanced at the door. She could get a quick peek at the frog, and nobody would ever know.

It was sneaky to look in someone's desk. But she wouldn't touch anything. Except the frog. Sam wouldn't care if she petted the frog. But he wouldn't find out anyway.

She hurried down the aisle to Sam's desk. The lid of the desk was raised up two inches. A book was holding it open. She could see the box inside the desk.

Amy looked around. She felt funny. She knew this was wrong. But she was too curious to stop. And the box was sitting right there.

She reached inside with two fingers and pulled out the box. She shook it gently. Something moved in there.

Amy opened the end of the box just a little and tried to peek inside. But she couldn't see anything. She opened the flap a little more. And a little more. Then she tipped up the box.

"Come on out, froggy," she said quietly. "I know you're in there." She moved the flap back and peeked inside.

A snake's head popped out of the box, about one inch from her eye.

"Yikes!" Amy said, dropping the box onto Sam's chair. She wasn't really afraid of snakes. But she'd been expecting a little frog.

The snake's head slid back inside the box. Amy looked at the box for a minute. She didn't want to touch it. But she couldn't leave it there on the chair.

She grabbed the box and pushed it back into the desk. The flap wasn't quite closed. But she didn't want to put her hand in there.

She ran out the door, then walked down the steps. She was still a little scared. She was never going to get into Sam's desk again. Not for anything.

The softball game had already started. Amy walked very slowly. Maybe she wouldn't have to play. Maybe they'd let her keep score.

"Here comes Amy," Fred yelled. "You guys have to take her."

"No way," another boy yelled. "We already

have all the other crummy players. You get her."

Amy hoped Mrs. Banks wouldn't stop the game and talk to the boys about being mean. That would make things even worse.

Amy hated softball.

Chapter Five

Mike ran across the playground. He liked playing softball. And he liked being outside where he didn't have to think about poems.

Sam had the ball. "Throw it here, Sam," Mike yelled. "Burn it in."

Sam threw the ball. Mike snagged it with his glove. "Don't worry, Sam," he said. "I won't tell anybody about Ernie."

"Ernie?" Brenda asked. "Who's Ernie?"

Mike groaned. Brenda had been right behind him. And he hadn't seen her.

Brenda came toward Sam. "Do you have another pet?"

"Ernie's my uncle," Sam said. He gave Mike a dirty look.

Mike laughed. "Yeah, we're talking about old Uncle Ernie." He threw the ball back to Sam. He'd almost done it again. He didn't mean to give away secrets. But things happened.

"I don't believe one word of that," Brenda said.

Sam turned away and threw the ball to Fred.

"He's got a pet, doesn't he?" Brenda asked quietly.

Mike looked around and saw his friend Greg standing by the backstop. "I've gotta see Greg," he said.

"He's got a pet," Brenda said. "I can tell."

Mike ran to the backstop. "How's it going, Greg?"

"Okay," Greg said. His voice sounded funny.

Mike looked at him. "Hey, Greg, is something wrong?"

"Everything's fine," Greg said. But Mike knew that wasn't true. Greg kept looking down at the ground.

"Did you see Sam's snake?" Mike asked. "It's really—" He stopped. But it was too late. He was giving away secrets again.

"Yeah, I saw it," Greg said.

Mike felt better. It wasn't giving away secrets if the other person already knew. "You sure you're okay?"

"I'm fine," Greg said, still looking down.

Mike looked down too. There was nothing on the ground. Then he looked at Greg's shoes. And looked again. On one foot Greg had a regular black shoe. On the other foot he had a black sneaker.

"Your shoes—" Mike started.

"Be quiet," Greg said. "I don't want everybody laughing at me."

"What happened?" Mike asked.

"I don't know," Greg said. "I didn't even notice until I was on the bus."

"It doesn't hurt anything."

"It looks dumb," Greg said. "Don't tell anybody."

"No problem," Mike said.

Greg moved away from the backstop. Mike didn't think it was a big deal. But Greg did.

Mrs. Banks didn't have them choose teams. She just split them into two groups. Mike liked that. He always felt sorry for the kids who were chosen last.

Mike's team was out in the field. Mike was playing second base. Greg ran way out into left field. Out there, nobody would see his shoes.

When the whole class played ball, they had special rules to speed up the game. The pitcher was somebody on your own team. So the pitcher always threw the ball easy. But you only got three pitches.

Carla was pitching to her team. Brenda was the first batter. She didn't swing at the first pitch.

"You might as well swing at it," Carla said. "It's a strike anyway."

"That's not fair," Brenda said. "I hate these stupid rules."

Carla put the ball right over the plate. Brenda started to swing, then stopped. "That was too high," she said.

"It was not," Carla said. "But that's still strike two. You better swing at the next one."

"Mrs. Banks," Brenda called, "these are stupid rules."

Mike saw Amy walking down the steps. He wondered what she'd been doing in the room so long. And she was taking her time walking out to the field.

Mike wasn't surprised. Amy wasn't very good at softball. She never got a bat on the ball.

"Here comes Amy," Fred called out. "You guys have to take her."

"No way," Trent said. "We already have all the other crummy players. You get her."

Mike looked over at Amy. She was acting like she hadn't heard them. But he knew she had.

Mike hated to have people feel bad. Especially somebody like Amy. Amy was always doing good things for people. And she'd been feeling sad ever since Sara moved away.

"Get a glove, Amy," Mrs. Banks called. "Your team's out in the field."

"Oh, man, that's not fair," Fred said. "Let her be on their team."

Mike saw Amy's face get red. "Shut up, Fred!" he yelled. "Amy's gonna get a hit today. You wait and see. She's got that mean-machine look in her eye."

Amy smiled and picked up a glove. She ran out to left field.

"Way to go, Amy," Mike yelled.

He hoped she wouldn't strike out again today.

Chapter Six

Amy ran out to left field. "Way to go, Amy," Mike yelled to her.

"You play up close," Greg told her. "I'll play back."

Amy hoped nobody hit a ball to her. She could catch a ball if somebody threw it. But it was harder when the ball was hit. Then it came too fast. And everybody was looking at you.

"Come on, batter," Mike yelled. "Give me some action, Jackson."

Amy smiled. Mike was her friend. He

never made people feel bad. She wished the other boys in the class were more like him. The girls, too.

Carla's team scored two runs. And the only ball hit to Amy was a slow grounder that stopped before it got to her. She picked it up and threw it in.

When Amy's team came in to bat, Mrs. Banks said, "Fielders bat first. Greg, you go first. Then Amy."

Fred let out a groan.

Amy looked over the bats and picked up the biggest one. With a big bat, it would be harder to miss the ball.

"Come on, Amy," Mike said. "Get a hit."

"I'll try," she said.

"You can do it. I've seen you use a hatchet at the garden shop. That's just like a bat."

"Not exactly," Amy said.

"Pretend you're holding a hatchet," Mike said. "And don't swing too hard. Just put the bat on the ball."

Greg hit the ball in the air. Two girls came to get it, but they both stopped. The ball fell between them. Greg ended up at second base.

"All right," Mike said to Amy, "get up there and swing that hatchet. Chop that old ball in half."

Fred was pitching for their team. "Why don't you just hold your bat out? Maybe I can hit it."

"Put it over the plate, Fred," Mike said. "She'll do all right."

"Here it comes," Fred said. Amy watched the ball sail toward her. When it got close, she swung the bat. She felt the ball hit her bat.

The ball bounced out in front of her. She stood and watched it roll.

"Run!" Mike yelled. "Run to first!"

Amy dropped the bat and ran toward first base. Sam ran in, picked up the ball, and threw it over the first baseman's head. The ball went rolling toward the soccer field.

Amy stopped running when her foot

touched first base. "Run to second," some-body yelled. Amy took off running again.

When Amy stopped at second base, she heard her team yelling, "Way to go, Amy" and "Good job." Greg had run all the way home.

Amy was amazed. It was great just to hit the ball and not strike out. But she had done even better. She had gotten on base and knocked in a run. What a fantastic day!

She stayed on second base while a boy struck out. She felt a little sorry for him.

Then Britt hit the ball into right field. Amy ran to third base, then ran home when Mike yelled, "Keep going!"

When Amy stepped on home plate, people clapped. Mike slapped her hand the way ballplayers on TV do. And even old Fred said, "Good going, Amy." Things couldn't get any better.

The game went on. Pretty soon Amy's team was back in the field. Then they were batting again. Amy thought her team was ahead, but she wasn't sure. The score didn't matter. She had gotten a hit and made a run.

"Game's over," Mrs. Banks called. Mike and Fred cheered, so Amy knew her team had won. That made things even better.

Mike came running up to her and slapped her hand again. "Way to go, slugger. I knew you could do it."

"That was fun," Amy said.

Fred ran past them. "We whipped 'em good," he said.

"Way to go," Mike shouted.

Fred slowed down. "Hey, Mike," he said, "you better be careful this period. You better not start blabbing and spoil the surprise party."

"Go fall in a hole," Mike said. "I won't tell."

"You better not," Fred said and ran on.

"That makes me mad," Amy said. "He's a big jerk."

She wished that Mike would get mad, too. But he just got quiet. "People think I can't keep secrets," he said after a minute. "I guess they're right."

"I don't think that," Amy said. "I trust you."

"That's good," Mike said, sounding sad. "But you better not tell me a secret."

"That's silly," Amy said. "I wouldn't be afraid to tell you a secret."

Mike's face got brighter. "Really?"

Amy was happy to see him smile again. "Sure. I know you wouldn't tell anybody if you promised not to."

An idea crossed Amy's mind. What if she told Mike a *real* secret? What if she told him about Mr. Warren? She had to tell somebody. She couldn't stand to keep it to herself any longer.

The smile slipped away from Mike's face. "I don't know," he said. "I might have an accident."

"I think you could keep a secret," Amy said.

Mike shrugged. "Maybe. Maybe not."

"I trust you," Amy said. "If you really want to—if you promise not to tell—you can keep a secret just like anybody else."

Mike smiled again. "I guess."

"I know you can," Amy said, talking faster. "I'm not afraid to tell you a secret. And this is something nobody in this school knows but me."

"Are you kidding?" Mike asked.

"No, I'm not kidding. This is a real secret. And you won't tell anybody, will you?"

Mike looked around for a second, then shook his head. "No, I won't tell. I promise."

"I believe you." For just a second Amy wondered if she was doing the right thing. But now that she was started, she couldn't stop. "Last Friday I came back to school late. I went to Mr. Warren's room to get a vase. And I saw him kissing Miss Dean. Isn't that neat?"

"Really?" Mike looked at her. "Are you sure?"

"I saw them."

"Maybe it wasn't what you thought," Mike said. "I saw an old movie like that. A girl was getting something out of a guy's eye. And somebody came along and thought—"

"She wasn't getting something out of his eye," Amy said. "She was kissing him."

"Wow," Mike said. "Mr. Warren and Miss Dean."

"I know you won't tell. I know I can trust you."

"Wow," Mike said again.

Chapter Seven

Mike walked toward the classroom very slowly. He felt good that Amy would trust him with her secret. And what a secret! Mr. Warren and Miss Dean!

Miss Dean was all right. She was always smiling and happy. If you wanted a girl-friend—and Mike didn't—Miss Dean would be okay.

But he had never thought about Mr. Warren having a girlfriend.

And now Mike was going to be in the same room with Mr. Warren. For the last period before lunch, Mrs. Banks taught math to Mr. Warren's class, and Mr. Warren taught English and reading to Mike's class.

Mike had to be careful. Mr. Warren always knew when Mike was hiding something. Like this morning. And now he was hiding two things.

Mike knew what to do. He'd go straight to his desk and get out his books. He'd stay busy all period. He wouldn't even look at Mr. Warren.

When Mike came in the door, Mr. Warren was erasing the chalkboard. Mike hurried past him, looking the other way.

"Hey, Mike," Sam whispered.

Mike looked back. "What do you want?"

Sam had all of the books out of his desk. "Ernie got loose," he said. "I can't find him."

"Oh no," Mike said. He looked under the desks around him. Then he got down on his knees.

Sam grabbed Mike's arm and pulled him

up. "Don't do that. Mr. Warren will want to know what you're looking for."

"Oh," Mike said. "I didn't think about that."

"We'll find him," Sam said. "Everybody's watching for him."

Mike sat at his desk and took out his English book. He held it in front of him while he looked around the floor. He didn't see Ernie anywhere. All he saw were shoes. Sneakers. Lace-ups. Boots.

Greg had his feet tucked clear back under his seat. Mike wished that Greg wouldn't worry so much. Who cared if your shoes didn't match?

"I need somebody to take a note to the office," Mr. Warren said.

People started waving their hands and saying, "Me, me."

"I'll do it," Mike called out. He loved going down the empty hallway and looking into the other rooms.

Mr. Warren looked past him. "Greg, could you do it for me?"

Greg's face turned red. "Could somebody else do it?"

People turned around and looked at Greg. They couldn't believe he didn't want to go.

Mr. Warren sent Britt instead. Mike looked over at Greg. He wished there was some way to help him.

Then Mike had an idea. Mike didn't care about shoes that didn't match. Why not trade shoes with Greg? Then Greg wouldn't have to worry.

Mike reached down and untied his shoes. Then he slipped them off. When Mr. Warren turned his back, Mike reached over and set his shoes on Brenda's desk.

"What are you doing?" Brenda asked.

"Hand those to Greg," Mike said.

"I don't want to touch those stinky things," Brenda said.

"Come on, Brenda. Hand them to Greg."

Brenda held her nose with one hand and picked up the shoes with the other.

"They don't stink," Mike said.

Mr. Warren came down the aisle. "Brenda," he said, "what are you doing?"

"It's not my fault," Brenda said. "Mike put his smelly shoes on my desk. He told me to give them to Greg."

Mr. Warren came and took Mike's shoes. Then he looked over at Greg. Greg had his feet tucked under his chair. "I've done the same thing, Greg," Mr. Warren said quietly.

"Look at that," Brenda said, loud enough for the whole school to hear. "Greg's shoes don't match at all."

So everybody had to come and look. Greg laughed and put his feet out in the aisle. But his face was bright red, and he didn't look at anybody.

"No big deal," Mr. Warren said. "Haven't you ever done that? I have. I got to school once and saw I had on a black shoe and a brown one. I told everybody it was the new style."

"I've done it too," Mike said. That wasn't true, but he wanted Greg to feel better.

Mr. Warren handed Mike his shoes. "Put 'em back on, Mike. Did you ever hear that old song?" He held out his arms and sang,

> *"Way down South in the land of cotton.*
> *My feet smell, but yours are rotten."*

Everybody laughed. Even Greg.

Mike smiled and pulled on his shoes. He didn't really feel like laughing. He had done it again. He had given away somebody's secret.

"Remember the scary story we read on Friday?" Mr. Warren said. "Think about the things that made it scary."

People began to call out answers:

"The spooky old house."

"It was dark."

"The lightning."

"The scary noises."

"Good," Mr. Warren said. "Can you think of anything else that was scary?"

"A snake!" Brenda yelled.

"A snake?" Mr. Warren said. "I don't remember a snake in the story."

"Not in the story," Brenda shouted. She was holding her feet off the floor. "Here. There's a dumb snake right over here."

Most people got up and headed for Brenda's desk. Some got up and went the other way.

"I hate snakes," Trent said.

"Can I pet him?" Carla asked.

"Why does everything have to happen to me?" Brenda moaned.

"Everybody move back," Mr. Warren said.

Sam pushed past the others. "I'll catch him for you."

"I'll get it," Mr. Warren said.

But Sam grabbed the snake behind the head and held it up. The snake wiggled, and lots of people said, "Ooooh."

Mr. Warren brought the wastebasket. "Put it in here, Sam."

Sam set the snake in the wastebasket.

"All right," Mr. Warren said, "you can all go back to your seats. If you want to see the snake, raise your hand. I'll bring it by."

Most people raised their hands. Not Mike. He didn't want Mr. Warren looking at him.

Mr. Warren took the snake around the room. Most people said, "Isn't he cute!" or "Can I pet him?" A few said, "Yuck" or "Ooooh."

"Can I take him home?" Nate asked. "My sister will jump through the ceiling."

Mr. Warren set the wastebasket in the corner and put some big books on the top. "Now," he said, standing by the front desk, "how did the snake get here?"

Nobody said anything. Mike felt his stomach get tight.

"Let's be detectives," Mr. Warren said. "Can snakes fly? Did it fly in through the window?"

People laughed and shook their heads.

"How do snakes get places?"

"They crawl," somebody said.

"Now, could the snake crawl into the room?" Some people shook their heads. "Why not?"

"It couldn't climb the steps," Trent said.

"And it couldn't open the door," Nate said.

"Exactly." Mr. Warren looked at the class. "And if the snake didn't come on its own, then there's only one answer left. Somebody brought it. And it wasn't me. And it wasn't Mrs. Banks. So who was it?"

Mr. Warren started looking at people one at a time. Mike didn't know what to do. If Mr. Warren saw his face, he'd probably know Mike was hiding something. But if Mike looked away, that would be worse.

But Mr. Warren wasn't looking at Mike. He

was looking straight at Sam. Mike knew Sam was in trouble. And he wanted to help. "It wasn't Sam," he yelled out. "He didn't bring the snake to school."

Everybody broke out laughing. Everybody but Sam. He shook his head and muttered, "I knew it."

Mr. Warren wasn't laughing, but he didn't look mad either. "Mike and Sam, come up here."

Mike got up slowly. It was the same old story. He had tried to help and made things worse.

"You did it again," Nate whispered.

Mike looked over at Sam. Maybe it wasn't too late. Maybe he could still help. "It wasn't Sam's snake," he called out. "It was mine. I was the one. I brought it to school."

"Forget it, Mike," Sam said. He had the Hot Tamales box in his hand. "Mr. Warren knows it was my snake."

Chapter Eight

While Mr. Warren was asking questions about the snake, Amy kept her head down. She was afraid to look him in the eye. The whole thing was her fault. She hadn't closed the box. So the snake had gotten loose, and the whole class was in trouble. And it was all because of her.

When Mr. Warren started looking at people, Amy got really scared. What if he looked at her? Would she be able to keep her face straight?

Then Mike shouted, "It wasn't Sam." And the whole class laughed.

Amy felt sorry for Mike. She knew he hadn't meant to tell on Sam. But now he and Sam were both in trouble.

"Take out your books," Mr. Warren said. "Read the story on page thirty-three." He picked up the wastebasket and went outside, along with Sam and Mike.

"Old Mike did it again," Nate said.

"They're in big-time trouble," Fred said.

Amy opened her book. But she was too upset to read anything. She was safe. Nobody would ever know that she let the snake get loose. But she felt awful. Mike and Sam were in trouble because of her.

She thought about going outside and telling Mr. Warren what she'd done. But it wouldn't do any good. Mike and Sam would still be in trouble.

Soon Mr. Warren came back into the room with the wastepaper basket. Amy could tell that the snake wasn't in it.

"You people know the rules," Mr. Warren

said. "No animals at school. If you break the rule, you go see Mrs. Sanchez."

Amy shivered. So Mike and Sam were going to the principal's office. All because of her.

"Has everybody finished reading the story?" Mr. Warren asked a few minutes later.

Two or three people said, "No."

"Take another minute," Mr. Warren said. "If you're done, think about how this story is different from Friday's story."

"We shouldn't have to read stories like this," Brenda said. "I'll bet I have nightmares tonight."

Amy looked down at her book. She hadn't even started to read. "What's the story about?" she whispered to Nate.

"This kid goes to sleep in a cave," Nate said. "Then a bear comes in."

Amy turned to the end of the story. She started to read about the bear. But she ended up thinking about Mike.

"All right," Mr. Warren said. "How are the two stories alike?"

"They're both rotten," Brenda muttered.

"Kids get scared," Britt said.

"Right," Mr. Warren said. "People are scared in both stories. Really scared. But is there a difference?"

"This guy has a good reason to be scared," Nate said. "The bear could eat him up. The people in the other story don't. They just get spooked by the noises."

"But people are scared just the same," Mr. Warren said. "Whether the danger is real or not."

The class went on talking about being scared and being in danger. Fred started to tell about being chased by a bull.

"Save that story, Fred," Mr. Warren said. "It's perfect for the writing we're going to do. I want each of you to write about a time you were scared. You can finish by saying whether or not you were in real danger."

"I'll do one about the roller coaster at the fair," Nate said.

"Hey, Brenda," Fred whispered, "you can write about being attacked by Sam's monster snake."

"You can write about looking in the mirror," Brenda said.

"What if you can't think of anything?" Carla asked. "I can't remember any times when I was scared."

Amy wished that was her trouble.

She decided to write about being in a car accident. She remembered the tires squealing and the horrible thump. Nobody had been hurt. But she still got chills when she thought about those sounds.

It was a lot easier to talk about dented fenders than about snakes in boxes. Or teachers kissing.

Afterward, people read their stories. Most of the stories were about real danger: a fire, getting lost in the mountains. And she read hers about the car wreck.

A few people told about scary times when there was no danger: Britt told about a monster movie. And Fred's bull had ended up licking his face.

Nate told about riding the roller coaster. "Was that real danger?" Mr. Warren asked the class.

"No," everybody said.

"Yes, it was," Nate said. "I could have been killed. And I almost had a heart attack besides."

Amy found herself watching Mr. Warren. But whenever he looked toward her, she looked away. In a way, she was scared of him. Which was silly. She knew there was no danger. But she still felt funny.

Mike and Sam came back to the room just before the lunch bell. "Tell us your story," Mr. Warren said. "I want people to know what happens if they bring an animal to school."

Mike and Sam stood in front of the class. They elbowed each other. They both said, "You go ahead."

Finally Sam said, "We took Ernie back to the bus stop. And we let him go."

"Too bad," Carla said.

"And we have to write reports on snakes," Mike said.

"And if we bring another animal to school," Sam added, "we get kicked out for a week."

Amy felt sorry for Mike. He'd gone to the principal, and he had to write a report. And he really hadn't done anything, except try to help.

She watched Mike walk back and flop down in his seat. She wanted to talk to him. She kind of wanted to tell him what she had done. But she wasn't sure about that.

As soon as the bell rang, she called over to him: "Hey, Mike, I want to talk to you."

Mike looked up and smiled. "Don't worry," he said. "I didn't tell anybody."

"What didn't you tell?" Brenda asked, loud enough for everybody to hear.

"What's going on?" Nate asked.

Brenda pointed at Amy. "Mike told her he didn't tell anybody. I think they have a secret."

"Not for long," Nate said. He turned to Amy. "Come on, Amy. You might as well tell us right now. We'll find out anyway."

Amy wanted to run. All kinds of people came crowding around.

"You won't find out from me," Mike called out. He pretended to zip his mouth. "My lip is zipped."

"He'll tell," Nate said. "Just wait."

Mike went running for the door. "No way."

Brenda moved up closer to Amy. "Was it a real secret?"

"You can tell us," Nate said.

"Yeah," somebody else said.

Amy wanted to move back. But her desk was in the way. "It's nothing," she said.

"You guys go on," Brenda said. "This is girl stuff."

"No problem," Nate said. "I'll find out from Mike." He headed for the door. Most of the others went with him.

"You can tell me, Amy," Brenda said.

Amy shook her head. "It's nobody's business."

Brenda snorted. "Well, you don't have to be that way. I don't care about your stupid secrets." She turned her back and walked away.

Amy picked up her lunch bag. She wished Sara hadn't moved away. She needed to talk to her.

Better yet, Amy wished she had moved away with Sara. She'd like to be in Arizona right now. Or anywhere else. Just so it was a long way from there.

Chapter Nine

"Hey, Mike," Nate said while they were eating lunch, "you might as well tell me. You know I can read your mind. It's about the party, isn't it?"

Mike tried to keep his face straight. "Forget it."

"It's about Mrs. Banks," Nate said. "It's about Sara. It's about Brenda. It's about Sam."

Mike moved his eyes on purpose. "Come on, Nate."

Nate laughed. "Okay, it's about Sam. You can tell me. It's about some animal, isn't it?"

Mike felt a little better. Nate couldn't read his mind. Not if Mike was careful.

"Amy already told me," Brenda said after lunch. "So it's not a secret anymore."

"Good try, Brenda," Mike said.

"Nate says you have a secret," Sam said. "I'll make you a deal. I'll tell you my secret if you tell me yours."

"I know that one," Mike said. "And you want me to go first, right? And then your secret is that you don't have a secret."

"Tell me what it starts with," Nate said. "Just give me the first letter."

"I know the secret," Fred said. "You've got a girlfriend."

"No way," Mike said.

"Then what is it?"

"It's none of your business."

"You've got a girlfriend. That's the secret. I can tell from your face."

By the time school was over, Mike was really tired. He hadn't told anybody anything. He was proud of that. But he was tired too.

So now everybody was going home. Except him. He had to go sit in Mr. Warren's room.

Amy was waiting outside their room. "Hi, Mike. I want to talk to you."

"I didn't tell anybody," he said. "They tried all kinds of stuff, but I didn't tell."

"I knew I could trust you," Amy said. "But that's not what I want to talk about." She looked around, then said, "I want to say I'm sorry."

"About what?"

"About you getting in trouble. It was my fault."

"What do you mean?"

"I looked in Sam's desk when everybody went to play softball. I thought he had a frog."

Mike laughed. "That's what I thought too. I guess you got a surprise."

"Yeah. I had my eye right up to the box, and out popped the snake. I don't think I screamed, but I might have." She smiled, then shook her head. "Anyway, I put the box back, but I guess it wasn't closed. So the snake got loose. And it's my fault you and Sam got in trouble. I'm sorry."

"It's okay." Mike didn't think it was Amy's fault. Sam was the one who brought a snake to school. But Amy looked worried. "Mrs. Sanchez wasn't mean or anything. She even petted Ernie."

Amy smiled at him. "Don't tell anybody what I did, all right?"

"I won't," Mike said.

Amy turned and headed down the steps. "See you tomorrow."

Mike walked down the hallway, shaking his head. Another secret! It was too much. He had too many secrets and too much homework. What a day!

He'd have to be very careful around Mr. Warren. Mr. Warren always knew when Mike was hiding something.

Mr. Warren's room was empty. And neat. Mr. Warren never had piles of books or papers on his desk. Mike wondered where he put everything.

Mike sat at a desk by the window. He had two books about snakes from the library. He could do a good report. But he also wanted to write a poem for Mr. Warren's party. That was harder.

Mike took out a piece of lined paper and wrote, "I hope you have a neat birthday." But that didn't sound like a poem. And he didn't know what to write next.

He sat and stared at the paper for a long time.

When Mr. Warren opened the door, Mike jumped. He had forgotten where he was.

"Hi, Mike," Mr. Warren said. "Do you have something to keep you busy?"

"I have too much to do," Mike said.

Mr. Warren sat at his desk. "I know how you feel."

After a minute Mike said, "I don't get it."

Mr. Warren looked up. "What's that?"

"I don't get how you write poems."

"Poems are just special ways of saying something," Mr. Warren said. "There's no right way to do them. You've done some good poems in our class."

"But I want to do one that sounds like a poem."

Mr. Warren smiled. "You mean like 'Twinkle, Twinkle, Little Star'?"

"Yes. That kind."

"Those aren't hard," Mr. Warren said. "Here's one way to do it. Stand up." Mike stood up. "Now march for me."

"What?"

"Pretend you're marching," Mr. Warren said. "Left, right. Left, right." Mike laughed while he marched. "Now I'll say one word with each step:

I know a boy. His name is Mike.
He likes to ride his mountain bike.

"I get it!" Mike shouted. He said the poem over again while he marched. Mr. Warren was right. It wasn't hard at all. Mike kept marching and said,

I am a boy. My name is Mike.
I used to ride a little trike.

"That's it," Mr. Warren said. "When you have big words, each syllable is one step. *Michael* is a two-step word." Mike tried that. "And *waterfall* is a three-step word."

Mike went left-right-left as he said, "Water-fall." Then he looked up at Mr. Warren. "I see how to do it now."

"That's just one kind of poem," Mr. Warren said.

"But that's the kind I want to do today," Mike said.

Mr. Warren smiled. "Sounds like you have something special going on."

Mike suddenly remembered why he was writing this poem. How could he have been so stupid—asking Mr. Warren about poems? Mr. Warren was still looking at him, so he had to say something.

"It's for my mother."

"That's great," Mr. Warren said. "Is this a special day?"

"Yeah. It's—" Mike tried to think of special days. All he could think of was Halloween, and that was six months away. "It's her birthday," he said finally.

"Is that right? When is it?"

"Tomorrow," Mike said. Mr. Warren was

still looking at him, so he went on, "She'll be thirty." But then he realized how stupid that was. Would Mr. Warren believe Mike's mother was exactly his age, with the same birthday? "Eight," Mike added. "She'll be thirty-eight."

"She doesn't look thirty-eight," Mr. Warren said.

"I'd better work on my poem," Mike said. When he sat down again, his hands were shaking. He had almost given away the secret. But he was safe now.

Mike took out a new piece of paper. He whispered words while he moved his feet. Then he wrote:

Happy birthday, Mr. Warren.
I hope you have lots of fun.
I hope you get lots of presents

Mike stopped writing and looked up. His feet kept marching, but he couldn't think of the right words.

"Are you having trouble?" Mr. Warren asked him.

"A little."

Mr. Warren smiled. "Why don't you read me what you have so far?"

Mike felt his face get hot. He didn't know what to do.

"It's okay," Mr. Warren said. "If your poem is for somebody special, you may not want anybody else to read it."

Mike couldn't believe it. Mr. Warren thought he was writing a poem to some girl. But Mike couldn't tell him the truth. "I can figure it out," he said.

"Sure you can." Mr. Warren winked at him.

"It's not a love poem," Mike said.

Mr. Warren laughed. "It's okay, Mike. You can write anything you want."

"It's not a love poem," Mike said again. But he could tell Mr. Warren didn't believe him. "It's a birthday—" He caught himself just in time and said, "It's for my mom's birthday."

Mr. Warren smiled and looked away. Mike didn't say any more. He hated having Mr. Warren think he was writing a love poem. But at least Mr. Warren wouldn't try to read it.

The classroom door opened, and Miss Dean came inside. Mike saw the way she smiled at Mr. Warren. Right then Mike knew Amy was right. Miss Dean had not been getting something out of Mr. Warren's eye. Mike wondered if Mr. Warren wrote poems for her.

"Hello, Mike," Miss Dean said.

Mike meant to say, "Hi, Miss Dean." But somehow it came out, "Hi, Kiss Dean." He bit his lip and slid down in his chair.

Miss Dean looked surprised for a second, then smiled. "Are you doing homework?"

Mike shook his head. He wanted to say, "I'm just writing this thing." But the words got mixed up in his mouth, and out came, "I'm just writing kiss thing."

Miss Dean gave him a funny look.

"It's a poem," Mike called out.

"That's nice. Can I read it?"

Mike didn't know what to do. He just sat and looked at her.

Mr. Warren whispered something to Miss Dean. She looked up and smiled at Mike.

Mike knew what they were thinking. They thought he was writing a poem about kissing. "I'm not writing a love poem," he said. His voice was louder than he wanted.

Mr. Warren and Miss Dean both smiled.

Mike knew they didn't believe him. He wanted to yell. But he bit his lip again.

Finally Mr. Warren said, "All right, Mike. You can go now. But no more kicking balls. We don't want people to get hurt. Okay?"

Mike nodded. But he didn't say a thing. He gathered up his snake books and his papers. He was afraid to say good-bye. What if it came out "Good-bye, Kister Warren?" So he just waved and went out the door.

Once he was in the hall, he began to laugh.

He was safe now. Then he put words to his footsteps: "I did not tell any secrets. Ha ha ha ha. Ho ho ho."

When Mike came down the steps, he heard Fred calling him: "Hey, Mike. Come on over here. I'll whip you in a game of horse."

"Just for a minute," Mike said.

Mike put down his books and ran to the basketball court. Fred had gone home and changed his clothes. Now he was wearing a Lakers top and some old blue shorts.

"I'll bet you told him about the party," Fred said.

"I'm not that stupid," Mike said.

"This is the world championship game of horse," Fred said. He threw Mike the ball. "Since I'm the champ, I'll let you go first."

Mike shot from the side and missed. Fred went to the free throw line and got ready to shoot.

Mike saw that Fred had a hole in the back of his shorts. It was the size of a golf ball.

Fred's shot went into the basket. "You have to make it from the line," Fred said.

Mike looked closer at Fred's shorts. "Do you have on pink underwear?" Mike asked him.

Fred stepped back. "What do you mean?"

"Look." Mike pointed to the hole. "I can see them."

Fred's face got red. "It's not my fault. My mom's in San Diego this week. My dad told me to wash the clothes. I put this red sweat shirt in, and it turned everything pink. I didn't know it would do that."

Mike started to laugh. "So you have pink underwear?"

"It's not funny," Fred said.

Mike kept laughing. "Fred and his pink undies."

Fred was *not* laughing. "You better be quiet," he said. "Let's play ball."

Mike didn't laugh anymore. Not while Fred was looking, anyway. But when he

thought about big old Fred with pink underwear, he could hardly hold it back.

After the game, he walked home. As he
walked, he made up poems:

> *I kicked the ball*
> *over the wall.*
> *We played horse.*
> *Fred won, of course.*

Then he thought about Fred and his pink
underpants. He laughed and started a new
poem:

> *If I tell about Fred,*
> *he'll break my head.*

Chapter Ten

Amy felt great. She had some special flowers for the party, and she had written a new poem.

Best of all, she'd heard from Sara. Yesterday a postcard had come with Sara's new address and the words "Please write to me. I'm lonesome." Amy didn't want her friend to be unhappy. But she was kind of glad Sara missed her.

Last night Amy had started a letter to Sara. She'd finish it tonight. She wanted to tell Sara all about the surprise party.

While Amy was fixing the flowers, Sam came in the door. She wondered if Mike had told him about the snake. Mike had promised he wouldn't. But he might have told by mistake.

Sam looked at the flowers. "Those are neat."

She watched Sam go down the aisle. He was her friend. She didn't like keeping secrets from him.

She was a little scared, but she went back to his desk. "Sam," she said, "I did something bad yesterday. I looked in your desk. I thought you had a frog."

Sam laughed. "Did Ernie scare you?"

"I jumped about three feet in the air. I wasn't expecting a snake. And then I don't think I closed the box all the way. So it was my fault he got loose. I'm sorry."

"That's okay."

"You're not mad?"

Sam shook his head. "You didn't do it on purpose." He smiled at her. "I'm glad you told me, though. I couldn't figure out how he escaped."

"I won't mess with your desk again," Amy said. "I promise."

"It doesn't matter," Sam said. "There's nothing in here but books and ratty papers."

Amy smiled as she went back to her desk. It was going to be a great day.

Mike came into the room. "I didn't tell," he called out. "I didn't spoil the surprise." He came walking by her desk. He stopped and whispered, "And I didn't tell anybody your secret either."

"I knew you wouldn't," Amy said. That wasn't quite true. But Mike didn't have to know that. "I told Sam about how I looked in his desk and left the box open."

"Good," Mike said. Then he laughed. "What's the matter? Can't you keep a secret?"

After the last bell, Mrs. Banks sent people out to her car. They brought back a cake and a punch bowl and boxes of party things. Crepe paper and punch cups and paper plates.

"The first thing we'll do," Mrs. Banks said, "is math."

Everybody moaned.

Mrs. Banks smiled. "I want each of you to put a problem on the board. And the answer to every problem will be—guess what number?"

"Thirty," Amy called out.

"That's right," Mrs. Banks said. "That's our magic number."

Most people wrote easy problems like 5×6 or 10+10+10. Nate wrote 29+1. Sam wrote 1+1+1+1 until he had thirty numbers.

Everybody helped string crepe paper around the room. Mrs. Banks moved all of the papers off her desk so that there was room for the punch bowl and the cake.

After the room was decorated, they all copied their poems onto special paper that Mrs. Banks had brought. "I did my own poem," Mike called out. "And nobody had to help me."

"What's the matter?" Nate said. "Didn't you like the one I wrote for you?"

Finally it was time to go outside. They played soccer that day, but it wasn't a very good game. Everybody kept looking over at the other field, where Mr. Warren's class was playing softball.

Amy thought soccer was worse than softball. People always ended up kicking each other. She stayed off to the side and ran only when the ball came close.

Then somebody kicked the ball out-of-bounds. It rolled toward the softball field. Amy trotted after it. But Mike was ahead of her. "I'll get it," he yelled.

The soccer ball rolled onto the softball field. One of the outfielders picked it up and threw it to Mike. Mike put the ball on the ground and kicked it back to the soccer field.

"Hey, Mike," Mr. Warren called out, "are you getting ready for birthday cake?"

Amy couldn't believe it. Mr. Warren knew about the party.

Mike's mouth dropped open. After a long, long time, he said, "What?"

"Isn't your mom going to have a birthday cake?" Mr. Warren asked.

Mike walked over to Mr. Warren. Amy moved that way too. She was being nosy. But she didn't care.

"It's not my mother's birthday," Mike said. "I just said that." He looked down at the ground. "I was writing a poem for a girl."

Mr. Warren smiled. "Hey, that's okay, Mike. I'll bet she likes it."

Amy turned and ran back to the soccer field. She couldn't believe it. Mike writing poems for a girl! That was as surprising as seeing the teachers kiss.

Who was the girl? She didn't think it could be her. But he had been nice to her lately.

But writing a poem?

When Mike came back to the soccer field, Fred ran over to him. "You didn't tell him about the party, did you?"

"No," Mike said.

"Next time I'll get the ball," Fred said.

"That's fine with me," said Mike.

Amy kept watching Mike. She wondered what he would say in a poem to a girl.

When the bell rang, everybody ran back to the classroom. They all stood by the door and waited.

"Let's be really quiet," Britt said. But people kept talking and laughing.

When Mr. Warren opened the door, they all yelled, "Surprise! Surprise!" Then they sang "Happy Birthday."

Mr. Warren looked really surprised. He kept shaking his head and laughing.

Mrs. Sanchez, the principal, came in the door. For a second Amy thought they were all in trouble. "I heard you have a cake down here," Mrs. Sanchez said. "And I'm starving to death."

Before they had their cake and punch, the class read their poems. Sam went first:

"I hope your birthday's cool.
Too bad you had to come to school."

Everybody laughed. But Mr. Warren said, "I can't think of anyplace I'd rather be."

All of the poems were good. One girl had written her poem in the shape of the number 30. Eight people had haiku poems. Amy was glad she had done a new one.

Carla did a list poem:

"On his birthday Mr. Warren dreams of:
Being tetherball champion,
Having everybody do their homework,
Catching a big fish,
Having a party,
Eating birthday cake,
Giving everybody in class an A."

Greg surprised them with a funny one:

"You might eat too much cake
And get a tummy ache.
So I'll be nice
And eat your slice."

Amy wished that she had written a funny poem. Last night she written a new one. But it wasn't funny at all. Her hands were shaking when she stood up to read:

"You're a neat teacher.
You help us to read.
You work on our writing

And teach what we need.
You always are friendly.
You know just what to say.
And now it's your birthday.
Have a really great day."

"What a fine poem," Mr. Warren said. "Thank you so much, Amy."

But then Fred said, "That ought to get you an A."

Amy slid into her seat. Why did people have to be mean?

"He's jealous," Brenda said.

And Carla said, "Be quiet, Fred. That was a good poem."

"I was just making a joke," Fred said.

Mike said he wanted to be last. When it was his turn, he stood up and looked around the room. "I wrote this poem last night. And I did it all by myself." Then he read:

"Happy birthday, Mr. Warren.
I hope you have lots of fun.

I hope you get lots of presents
And you like every one.
Happy birthday, Mr. Warren.
I hope you feel like a king.
People thought I'd tell your secret,
But I did not say one thing."

Mike bowed, and everybody laughed. "That's right," Mr. Warren said. "This was a complete surprise."

"And I wasn't writing a poem for a girl," Mike shouted.

Some people laughed. Some said, "What's he talking about?"

Mr. Warren smiled. "Mike had to trick me to keep from spoiling the surprise."

"See?" Mike said to the class. "I kept the secret."

Amy was glad in a way. It hadn't seemed right for Mike to be writing poems for a girl. But she still wondered what his poem would have said.

Everybody had punch and cake. When

Amy got her cake, Mrs. Sanchez told her, "I enjoyed your poem very much."

Two girls from Mr. Warren's class came through the door. "Mr. Warren," they called out, "we need you back in our room."

"I'll be there in two minutes," Mr. Warren said. He raised his hand. "Would you take your seats? I have something to say."

"We get double homework tomorrow," Sam said.

Mr. Warren waved him away. "What a great party! I loved all of your poems. Thank you very much. I don't know how you kept this a secret."

"Hey," Nate said, "we can keep a secret."

"Yes, you can," Mr. Warren said. "And I have another one for you. Only, from now on, it's not a secret." He looked at them and smiled. "This summer Miss Dean and I are getting married."

Everybody started talking at once, saying "Wow" and "That's great."

One boy said, "Foo. I wanted to marry Miss Dean."

Mr. Warren held up his hand. "We weren't going to tell anybody for a while. But somebody found out by accident. I want to thank her for keeping it a secret and letting me be the one to tell the good news." He looked straight at Amy, then smiled and winked.

The whole class turned and looked at her.

"I have to go back to my room," Mr. Warren said. "I think I may be having another party. Thanks for everything. I hope you'll help me out by finishing this cake."

Some of the boys headed for the front desk. When Mike came past, he whispered, "Don't worry. I'll never tell."

Amy leaned back in her seat and smiled. She had a lot of things to put into that letter to Sara.

Chapter Eleven

Mike sat at his desk, eating his second piece of cake. Mrs. Sanchez had cut the cake into small pieces so that everybody could have seconds.

Trent couldn't eat sugar, so Mrs. Banks had brought a diet soda for him. But Fred had Trent get punch and cake anyway. So Fred had double helpings. "I need extra food," he said. "I'm a growing boy."

Mike was very happy. Everybody had liked his poem. And he hadn't spoiled the surprise party. He had showed that he *could* keep a secret. Especially if it was important.

Even so, he was glad that he didn't have any more secrets. He didn't have to be careful now. But then he looked over at Fred eating his extra cake.

Well, there was one secret left.

While Mike ate, his feet started to march. In his mind, he began a new poem:

> *I did not tell any secrets.*
> *They said I would, but I don't care.*
> *I can keep any secret,*
> *Except about Fred's underwear.*

Mike looked around the room. He saw Amy sitting by herself. She was his friend. And with Sara gone, she needed a laugh.

"Hey, Amy," he called out, "I have something to tell you."